WILD HORSES

WILD HORSES

written and illustrated by **Glen Rounds**

Holiday House/New York

The Red Desert is a barren land of high rocky ridges and dusty sagebrush flats, where men seldom go. For the greater part of the year the grass there is dry and sparse and the few waterholes far apart. Life is difficult for the wild horses that make this place their home.

But spring, with its warm days and melting snow,
brings new grass and easier time.

Then the wild horses spend long hours greedily searching out the first green patches that appear on sunny slopes and flats.

Spring is also the time of new colts, and the horses gather to sniff and inspect each new addition to the band.

But they make their introductions circumspectly,
for any who venture too close risk punishment from
the mare's teeth or hoofs.

The older horses spend the cool morning hours grazing, while the colts gather in small playful groups under the watchful eye of one or another of the old mares always standing guard on some nearby bit of high ground.

But when the sun is high, the band leaves off its grazing and
climbs to some high ridge where there will be a small
breeze to blow away the flies.

And there the horses doze the hot midday hours away.

Spring and early summer is also the time of year when the horse hunters sometimes find their way into the wild-horse range. But the first sight of distant riders

brings a shrill alarm whinny from the mare on lookout, and the
entire band quickly bunches for flight.

To escape these men mounted on fast horses and swinging long
catchropes, the wild horses pour recklessly down steep slopes
and along knife-edge ridges where riders hesitate to follow.

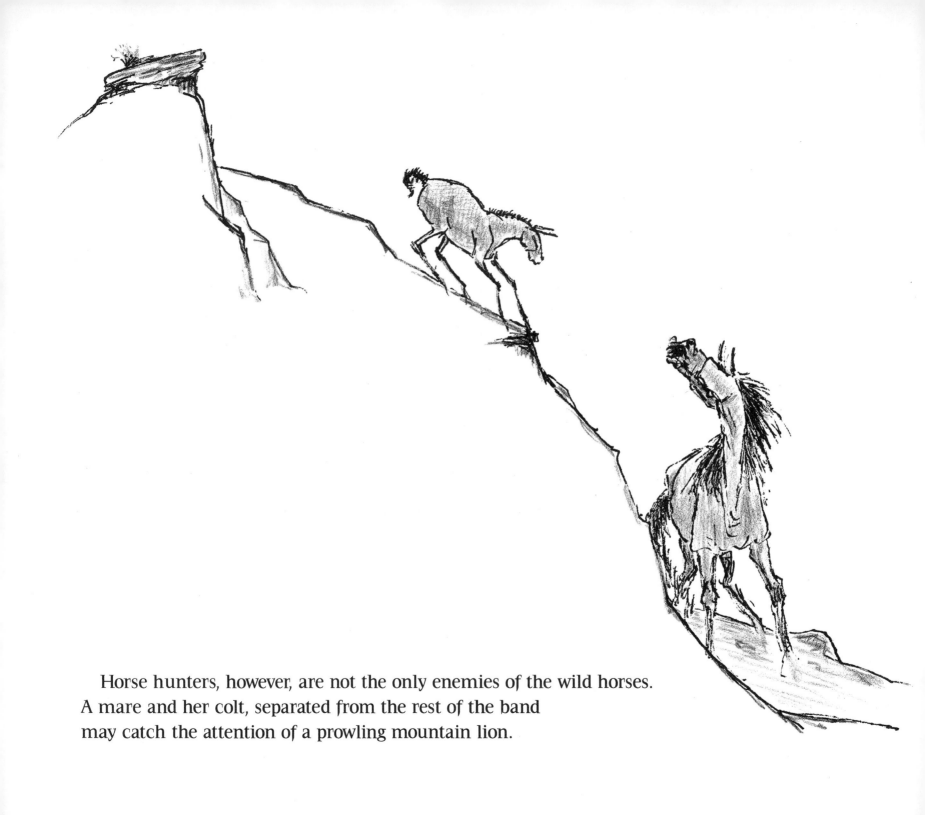

Horse hunters, however, are not the only enemies of the wild horses.
A mare and her colt, separated from the rest of the band
may catch the attention of a prowling mountain lion.

A hunting wolf will sometimes try to stampede a lone mare,
in hopes of separating her from her colt.

But if she stands her ground, he will usually go off
in search of smaller game rather than face the
danger from her teeth and hoofs.

By the middle of summer the hot winds begin to blow across
the Red Desert, shriveling the grass and drying up the
scattered waterholes one after another.

The distance the wild horses must travel between grass and
water becomes so great that in the driest times they may drink only
every second or third day.

Since they are still nursing, the colts find the waterholes more entertaining than useful and spend their time splashing about in the muddy water or rearing in mock fright at dragonflies, frogs and water snakes.

Winter comes early to the Red Desert. But the wild horses will have already grown thick shaggy coats of long winter hair.

During the first small snowstorms the colts sniff
and snort at the strangeness of the lazily drifting
flakes, or buck and run to dislodge the clinging stuff
from their backs.

But later the great blizzards bring bitter cold and snow
that blows in blinding clouds for days on end.
Then the wild horses turn their tails to the wind and,
crowding together for warmth, sleep standing up.

Then, when the weather clears, they leave the deep
drifted flats to search the high windswept ridges
for patches of grass blown clear of snow.

But spring finally comes again, and with the first warm days
the wild horses everywhere begin to rub and scratch to relieve
the itching of their hides as their winter coats loosen
and come away in great ragged tufts.

And before the new grass is fetlock high, they will have lost their lean winter look and once more be sleek and fat.

There was a time when wild horses by the thousands could be found on the Western plains. But, as the country was settled, the ranchers began systematically to exterminate the wild bands, as they had the buffalo, to save the grass and water for their growing herds of beef.

At first the wild horses were simply shot on sight, but later, professional wild-horse hunters made a profitable business of shipping them by the trainload to the dog food factories in the East.

So today, only a few scattered bands remain — driven far back into Badlands areas too barren or inaccessible to be of use to the ranchers. The Red Desert might be such a place.

— GLEN ROUNDS

WILD HORSES is an abridgement of WILD HORSES OF THE RED DESERT written and illustrated by Glen Rounds, which was published by Holiday House as a 48 page book in 1969.

Library of Congress Cataloging-in-Publication Data
Rounds, Glen, 1906–
Wild horses / written and illustrated by Glen Rounds.
p. cm.
Abridged ed. of: Wild horses of the Red Desert. 1969.
Summary: Traces the season-to-season activities of a band of wild horses as they raise their young, evade enemies, and survive the rigors of their badlands home.
ISBN 0-8234-1019-6
1. Wild horses—Juvenile literature. [1. Wild horses. 2. Horses.] I. Rounds, Glen, 1906–
Wild horses of the Red Desert. II. Title.
SF360.R68 1993 92-73608 CIP AC
599.72'5—dc20